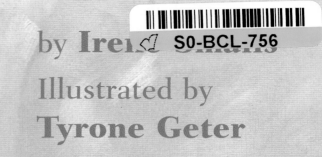

by **Irene Smalls**

Illustrated by
Tyrone Geter

Little, Brown and Company
Boston New York Toronto London

Irene and the
Big, Fine Nickel

For Louise and for Harlem

First Paperback Edition

Library of Congress Cataloging-in-Publication Data

Smalls, Irene Jennie.
  Irene and the big, fine nickel / by Irene Smalls, illustrated
by Tyrone Geter.
    p.   cm.
    Summary: Relates the adventures of a young girl, living in Harlem
in the 1950s, on the morning that she finds a nickel in the street.
    ISBN 0-316-79898-3 (pb)
    [1. Atro-Americans — Fiction.   2. Harlem (New York, NY) —
Fiction.]   I. Geter, Tyrone, ill.   II. Title.
PZ7.S63915Ir   1991   89-32816
[E] — dc20

10 9 8 7 6 5 4 3 2 1

Published simultaneously in Canada
by Little, Brown & Company (Canada) Limited
and in Great Britain by Little, Brown & Company (UK) Limited

Harlem was a place where nobody locked the door, and you never questioned being black because there were a million people who looked just like you. *"I Love You, Black Child."*

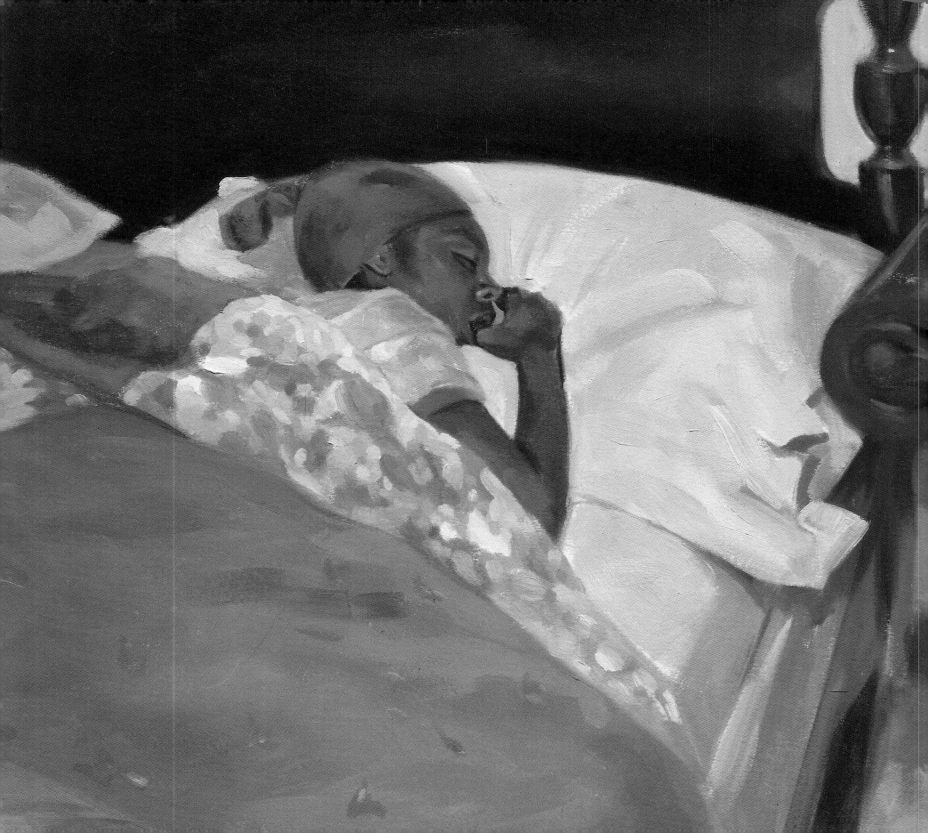

Irene had had her special dream again, but the rays of the morning sun from the alley window pushed the dream out of her mind. It was early morning, and the music came softly slipping through the window.

The music came from the radios and stereos that were constantly going. Irene could hear Mrs. Joyner's Mahalia Jackson record and Brown Betty's Billie Holiday singing "God Bless the Child." Irene always liked morning especially because no one could sing the one song she didn't like, "Good night, Irene, good night, Irene, I'll see you in my dreams."

It was time to get up. It was Saturday, and her godmother had come and taken the younger kids, Yvonne, Peanut, and Hazel, so Irene was traveling solo. Mommy was still sleeping. Irene could hear her snoring in the front bedroom of the railroad apartment. So Irene would get her own self up.

Irene started moving her body. Okay, brown toes, time to wake up. Okay, brown legs, okay, bum-bum, tummy, arms. Irene stretched her sturdy caramel frame. She took the stocking cap off her head as she got out of the bed she shared with her sisters and brother and went into the kitchen. Irene moved the board that covered the bathtub and started to wash up. All of a sudden it hit Irene that today was the day that Lulamae's mother made banana pudding. She put on her clothes in a flash. Irene was seven and very independent. She opened the door and walked down the green hallway past the toilet room. She walked across the white tiled floor to the door of Miss Sally's apartment to see Lulabelle and Lulamae.

Lulabelle and Lulamae were Irene's best friends. They had come up north to Harlem from the same town in South Carolina that Irene's people were from.

Irene opened the door and went in. Nobody was up. "I guess the banana pudding's not started yet." So Irene helped herself to a drop biscuit from the plate on the table. Irene liked going to Miss Sally's. At Miss Sally's house, with thirteen kids, there was always something going on. Irene heard a noise, and li'l brother came into the kitchen. "I got tired of sleeping," he said. Li'l brother's eyes watched as each morsel of drop biscuit reached Irene's mouth. "There's more biscuits on the table," Irene protested. But li'l brother wanted a bite of Irene's biscuit.

Children, Irene thought, but Godmother said that you were supposed to be polite and share, even with li'l brothers.

"Here," Irene said grudgingly as she held out her biscuit. Li'l brother smiled and took the biggest bite that his mouth could hold. "Save me a little," Irene said.

"Okay," li'l brother said in a biscuity voice.

Miss Sally came into the kitchen. "Good morning, Miss Sally," Irene said.

"Morning, chile," Miss Sally said.

Miss Sally chuckled. She knew that Irene had come looking for banana pudding. "Puddin' not ready yet. Should be done 'bout suppertime, though." She continued, "Lulabelle and Lulamae's not up yet."

"Well, please tell them I'll be back, and thank you for the biscuits," Irene said.

"That's just fine, chile," Miss Sally said.

Irene got up and walked out the door and down the long hallway to the white marble steps. She hopped down the steps to the doorway.

Harlem was just waking up, and Irene pretty much had the street to herself. As she came out, Irene saw Charlene. Irene walked over to Charlene.

"Morning, Charlene," Irene said.

Charlene's people came from the Geechee Islands down south, and they were church people. "Praise the Lord," Charlene said.

"Do you want to play?" Irene asked. Charlene nodded, held up her hands to play, and joined Irene singing, "Down down, baby, down down the roller coaster, sweet sweet baby, I'll never let you go. Shimmy shimmy coco ba, shimmy shimmy ba."

RUBENSTEIN'S
FRESH MEAT-VEGETABLES
USED
HARLEM
401
FRESH FISH!!
6¢ PER lb.
SUGAR 22¢
BACON 12¢
OKRA
FISH

As the girls were playing, the streets started to come alive. Mr. Rubenstein, the Jewish grocer across the street, started opening up his store. The record shop on Eighth Avenue opened and started playing the new James Brown record: "This is a man's world, but it would be nothing without a woman or a girl."

Their hand game ended, the girls started teasing each other, playing the dozens.

Irene said, "Your eyes may shine, your teeth may grit, but better looking is one thing that you will never get."

Charlene didn't like that, so she said meanly, "Yo' momma."

Now, everybody knows that you don't mess around with calling names of people's momma! Irene didn't play that. Irene was ready to fight. Charlene just stood still, wary, watching Irene.

"You stay right here, I'll be right back."

Irene raced upstairs to her apartment and braided her hair tightly. Charlene wasn't going to pull her hair out. Then Irene greased her face, neck, and arms with Vaseline from the big jar on the bureau. Charlene wasn't going to scratch up her face, either. Irene flew back down the steps. She was ready like Freddy. Irene looked up and down the street. No Charlene.

Hmm. Oh well, Irene thought, Godmother always said that ladies didn't fight unless they had to.

Irene rubbed the Vaseline from her face and neck onto her legs. Godmother told her to do that to keep her skin from getting ashy, so that she would have soft skin when she got older. Older seemed so far away. The absolute limit to human existence to Irene was being in the seventh grade.

"Well," Irene said, "I might as well go and check and see if Lulabelle and Lulamae are up yet."

As Irene walked into Miss Sally's apartment, the girls were finishing up their drop biscuits with jam. Miss Sally had finished cooking the bacon for Mr. Sally's breakfast and was saving the grease to make soap later on.

"Morning, Irene," Lulabelle and Lulamae said as they saw Irene. Even though the girls had come up north when they were babies, they still spoke with a lingering drawl. They were the color of dark chocolate, with long arms and legs and short kinky hair that their mother, depending on their inclination, would cornrow or press with a hot comb.

"Want to go out and play?" Irene asked.

"Can we, Momma?" Lulabelle said.

Lulamae rubbed the last bit of sleep out of her eyes. Her hair was matted down, and her long arms stuck out of the too-short pajamas that Mr. Sally had brought from the white people in the Bronx. Lulamae looked at her mother hopefully.

"Okay, chillun, you wash on up and go on outside." Miss Sally went to give Mr. Sally his breakfast and get the rest of her brood moving.

Lulabelle pushed the board back over the bathtub in the kitchen as her sister started to wash up. Lulamae, as she was brushing her teeth, gave a whistle. She had a big gap between her two front teeth that made the best whistle. She was the envy of all the girls in the neighborhood.

"Let's go climbing," Irene said. The two girls quickly dressed, and together they and Irene headed for Colonial Park. Irene hiked up her skirt and scrambled over big rocks to reach the top of the rocks.

"Let's go down," Lulamae said. She didn't like high spots too much.

"Sure," Lulabelle and Irene said. They raced down the rock and took a long jump over the fence to the grass. Down in the grass, Irene spied a box. "C'mon, let's get some dirt for our plants."

Irene had sent for some seeds from a comic book, and she was going to grow a garden on the fire escape.

"Let's dig a hole to China," Irene said, and the girls pretended that they were digging a hole to the center of the earth. As the box filled up, the girls slowed down. Lulabelle said, "We can go to China another day."

Carefully the girls carried the box filled with dirt across Bradhurst Avenue and up to the doorway of 320 West 147th Street. They carried the box upstairs and carefully placed it on the fire escape. Irene ran under her bed and got the seeds as Lulabelle got a plastic cup full of water. Irene poked half a finger in the soil and dropped in a seed as Lulamae smoothed each seed hole over. Lulabelle poured on the water. "Let's go play hide-and-seek next," Lulabelle said.

"Girl, first let me tell you about Charlene," Irene said. "She was acting so silly this morning. She said to me, just 'cause I was teasing her a little bit, 'Yo' momma.'"

Lulabelle and Lulamae agreed Charlene must have plumb lost her mind.

"Godmother said there's no explaining some folks," Irene concluded.

The three girls ran out of the apartment and down the stairs of the gray stone tenement building. As they walked out into the street, Irene noticed something in the gutter. The gutters of the street were so clean that you never saw anything in them, but this time there was definitely *something* there.

"Wow, this must be my best day ever," Irene said. It was a nickel.

"Land sakes a'mighty," Lulabelle said.

The girls were overwhelmed at their good fortune. Irene ran over and grabbed the nickel. A whole nickel! It burned hot and rich in her hand. This nickel was enough to buy a raisin biscuit from the West Indian bakery. The girls hopscotched with joy to the corner and then made the turn to the bakery door.

The big nickel felt so heavy in Irene's hand. She had the high honor of holding it, since she was the one who had seen it first.

"Miss Susie, Miss Susie," Lulabelle and Irene said in one breath.

"Rest your nerves, chile. I'll get to you in a minute," Miss Susie said.

Miss Susie waited on her other customers, and finally the girls' turn came.

"Miss Susie, we have a nickel, and we would like to buy the biggest raisin bun you have," the three girls said in one big rush.

"Rest easy, children. Your life's long but you're foolish with it. Take it easy, I'll give you a nice raisin bun and maybe a little extry," Miss Susie said to the three beaming brown faces.

It's a lucky day today, Irene thought. "How's Nathaniel?" Irene said. Nathaniel was Miss Susie's son. He was only a boy, but Irene was told always to be polite.

"Oh, he's in the back, baking with his daddy."

Miss Susie handed the girls the bag with the raisin bun plus.

"Thank you, ma'am," the girls said.

"Let me hold it," Lulabelle said. Miss Susie handed the bag to Lulabelle. Lulabelle handed the bag to Irene. Irene held the bag high and proud and walked around the corner. Lulabelle and Lulamae scooted right behind. Irene sat down on the curb. The girls sat on either side. All three girls studied the curb intently, but this time there was no nickel to be found.

"Here comes ole scuzzy Charlene," Lulamae said.

Irene didn't move. She kept looking at the raisin bun.

"Hi," said Charlene. "Seems like a mighty fine day," she said, looking at Irene.

"Suppose it is," Irene said.

"Raisin bun sure looks good. I sure would like a piece," Charlene said quietly.

Lulabelle made a face.

Irene turned to face Charlene for the first time. Charlene flashed a broad smile.

"God don't love ugly, bein' mean and fightin' is not the best thing to do," Irene's godmother always told her.

Irene paused for a moment. "S'pose you could have a piece," Irene said. Charlene settled in on the curb next to Lulabelle.

"Let's eat the crumbs first, and then we'll eat the raisin bun," Irene said.

Raisin bun can sure taste good on a happy day with your three best friends. And to think the day had just begun! There was Miss Sally's banana pudding to be eaten before the day ended. Irene was feeling seven and in heaven on this summer day in Harlem.